P9-CBQ-299

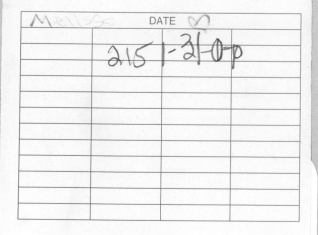

Melissa	DATE ♡		
215	1-3/0 p		

Fine Feathered Friends

Poems for Young People by *Jane Yolen*

Photographs by
Jason Stemple

WORDSONG ✦ BOYDS MILLS PRESS

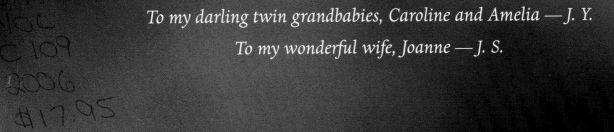

To my darling twin grandbabies, Caroline and Amelia — J. Y.

To my wonderful wife, Joanne — J. S.

Text copyright © 2004 by Jane Yolen
Photographs copyright © 2004 by Jason Stemple
All rights reserved

Published by Wordsong
Boyds Mills Press, Inc.
A Highlights Company
815 Church Street
Honesdale, Pennsylvania 18431
Printed in China

Visit our Web site at www.boydsmillspress.com

10 9 8 7 6 5 4 3 2

Library of Congress Cataloging-in-Publication Data

Yolen, Jane.
  Fine feathered friends : poems for young people / by Jane Yolen ;
photographs by Jason Stemple.— 1st ed.
   p.   cm.
ISBN 1-59078-193-7 (alk. paper)
1. Birds—Juvenile poetry. 2. Children's poetry, American.
[1.Birds—Poetry. 2. American poetry.] I. Stemple, Jason, ill. II. Title.

PS3575.O43F56 2004
811'.54—dc22

2003026791

First edition, 2004
Book designed by Jason Thorne
The text of this book is set in 18-point Dante.

Front cover: red-bellied woodpecker (Melanerpes carolinus);
back cover: yellow-crowned night heron (Nyctanassa violacea);
page 1: western meadowlark (Sturnella neglecta);
page 2: green-tailed towhee (Pipilo chlorurus);
page 4: little blue heron (immature) (Egretta caerulea).

Contents

Bird Watcher:
A Note from the Author

Going out for a drive with the Yolen-Stemple family can be a slow process. We stop for birds.

I don't mean birds crossing the road. I mean birds on the road, above the road, in the trees, on the ground, swimming, fishing, strolling, flying. Birds everywhere.

My husband, David, is a bird watcher. Growing up in the West Virginia woods, he saw a lot of them. I grew up in New York City. Bird watching for me consisted of pigeon, not-pigeon. I was an adult before I learned to look at birds.

Our three children, including Jason, the youngest, learned to identify birds from the time they were toddlers, going owling with their father or stopping frequently on our road trips to watch whatever avian creatures happened to come our way.

Jason's interest in birds turned to sketching and drawing them on paper. Then he became fascinated with cameras. Soon he was taking photos of wildlife. But over time he developed a talent for—and specialized in—photographing birds. Since he has lived in Massachusetts, Colorado, and now Charleston, South Carolina, and has traveled widely in the United States, he has photographs of many different kinds of birds. We used a number of them in our first bird book together, *Wild Wings*. But Jason had more than enough wonderful photos for this second book.

Each picture he sent me over a period of a year spoke a different poem in my head. Some mimic the birds' motions or songs. Some comment on the birds' feeding habits or way of walking, or their coloration or behavior. And if you look at the pictures and read about the birds, you can write poems for these photographs, too.

Why Does?

Why does a red-winged blackbird sing
From a stalk of grass at the start of spring?
Does he sing for a mate, for a nest full of eggs?
Does he sing with a spring in his wings and his legs?
Does he sing for his place, for the grace of sky,
For the fact of the food that lies nearby?

Or does he only sing in praise
Of blackbird kind and blackbird ways?

The red-winged blackbird (Agelaius phoeniceus) *can be found in marshes and open fields. Great flocks of these birds, roosting and feeding together, patrol grain fields and help destroy crop-feeding insects. The male's shoulder patch is like a brilliant military epaulet.*

Barred Owlet

Like a rag doll
sewn from remnants,
owlet flops
upon his perch.
The hidden ears you cannot
see
he uses in his mealtime
search.

And like a rag doll
sewn from remnants,
owlet has
black button
eyes.
His feathers look
like bits of cloth.
They keep him quiet
when he
flies.

For then he goes
as soft as
night
and comes alive
in silent
flight.

As an adult, the big gray-brown barred owl (Strix varia) is graceful and buoyant in flight. It lives in swamps and in deep-wooded areas, preferring to roost in tree hollows, although it has been known to take over the nest of a hawk or crow or even a squirrel's old nest.

Mute Swan: A Haiku

Solitary swan,
More still than its photograph,
Finally moves on.

The mute swan (Cygnus olor) *almost always swims with an S curve
in its neck, its orange bill pointing down toward the water. This bird
originally was brought from the Old World and is most often seen in
parks. Though it can make a variety of hisses and grunts, it is
usually silent, hence its name.*

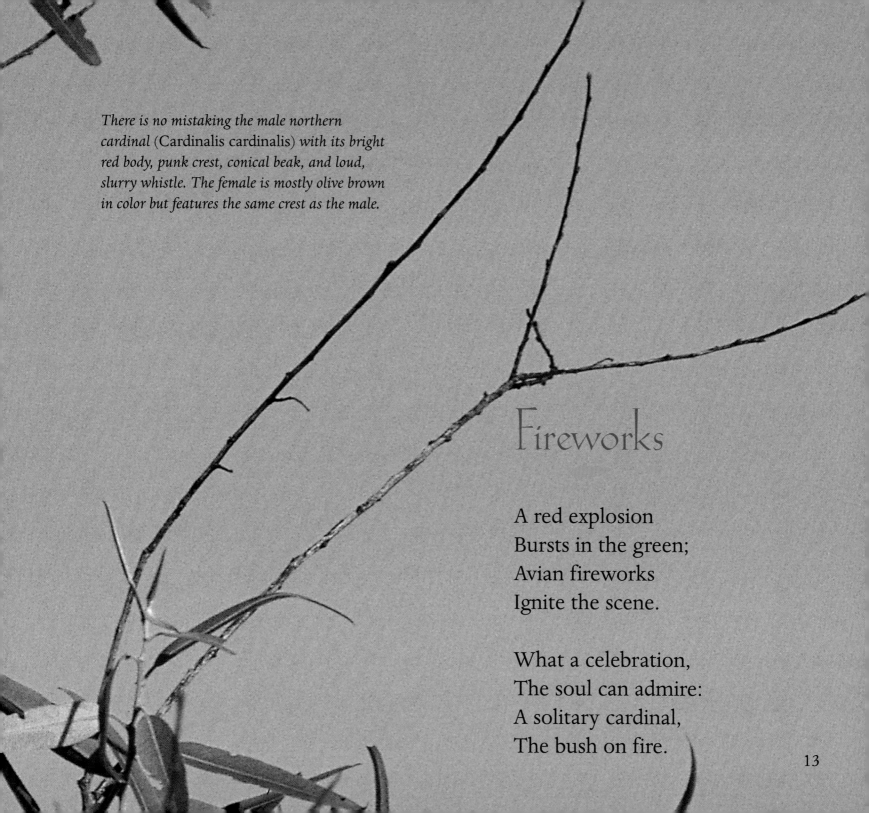

There is no mistaking the male northern cardinal (Cardinalis cardinalis) with its bright red body, punk crest, conical beak, and loud, slurry whistle. The female is mostly olive brown in color but features the same crest as the male.

Fireworks

A red explosion
Bursts in the green;
Avian fireworks
Ignite the scene.

What a celebration,
The soul can admire:
A solitary cardinal,
The bush on fire.

Pelican Meals

A pelican strains
to eat his meals.
I wonder how
a pelican feels
when fish go wiggling
in his beak,
which makes it very
hard to speak.

The American white pelican (Pelecanus erythrorhynchos) is a member of the Pelecaniformes order, the only group of birds whose feet are covered by a web of skin that wraps all the way around the back toe as well as the front ones. Descendants of birds that lived during the Cretaceous period, about 100 million years ago, pelicans have huge skin pouches under their beaks that serve as strainers.

16

Dove in Winter

Breast against the icy wire,
Winter dove in gray attire,
Fends for self, this solo flyer,
All alone, in single choir.

Pressed against the icy briar,
Fence so cold it feels like fire.
"Hallelujah," coos the crier.
Wisdom cautions to retire.

*The commonest and most abundant of native American doves, the mourning dove (*Zenaida macroura*) is found year-round on farmlands as well as in the suburbs. It is one of those birds that has benefited from human activity, living easily on weed seed, waste grains, and cultivated pastureland.*

"Sea Parrot"

What sailor, on what long sea trip,
Invented that most famous quip
And called the puffins this new name?
The birds will never be the same.
They swim with ease below the waves,
Their diving skills win highest raves.
Upon their toes they nimbly walk,
But unlike parrots, never talk.
So why did sailors name them so?
It's something we shall never know.

The Atlantic puffin (Fratercula arctica) is easily identified by its astonishing triangular-shaped orange, yellow, and steel blue bill. The male uses it as a pickax to dig its burrow at the top of a cliff for the female to lay her eggs.

Junco Perching

The junco sits,
surveys the field,
for any seeds
the land will yield.
A life well lived,
a perch well sat,
the junco needs
no more than that.
Shadow perched
on shadow limb—
hosannas red,
a graying hymn.

The dark-eyed junco (Junco hyemalis) is a small gray and white bird that lives in coniferous and mixed forests. Its range is enormous—from Mexico to Alaska and all the way east across North America to Newfoundland. Easy to spot, either perching or feeding on the ground, it eats both seeds and insects. The Oregon junco and the white-winged junco are just two of several kinds of juncos.

Osprey

Perch lover,
Wind hover,
Air beater,
Fish eater.
Strike in the water,
And carry the prey home.

Egg bearer,
Nest carer,
Strong breeder,
Young feeder.
Strike in the water,
And carry the prey home.

The osprey (Pandion haliaetus) *is an eagle-like
hawk that loves water. A fish eater, it hovers on
beating wings over a river or lake, spots its prey,
and then dives down, enormous feet first, to grab
its unsuspecting meal.*

23

Gambel's quail (Callipepla gambelii), *named after naturalist William Gambel, is a chunky-bodied bird with a plume on its head. Found almost exclusively in the southwestern United States, Gambel's quail is a fast runner but not much of a flier. It takes flight only to escape danger or to get up to its roost at night. Bobcats and human hunters are among its worst enemies. A covey—a group of quail—can range between twelve and twenty-four birds.*

24

Gamboling Gambel

I'd rather walk through the long dry grasses
That shudder and shake when the hot wind passes
Than take to the air, my wings hard pumping
Except when the bobcat is snarling and jumping.

I'd rather stroll on the hot desert sand
Than make my way on the cooler land,
Gamboling along, my roost near by,
My cover, earth and grass, not sky.

I'd rather run on the low desert range,
Where shadows of scrub don't seem so strange,
Where familiar thickets offer me a hide
When the dangers are many and the world's too wide.

I'd rather walk, my covey close at hand,
On this brown and gray and beautiful dry land.

Roadrunner

A bit of wind, a dash of snow,
His speedy legs now go too slow.
A sudden freeze, a skin of ice,
His feathers pump and plump up twice.
A touch of chill, a sneeze or three,
He's changing unexpectedly.
A dash of cold, of winter sign,
Roadrunner's now a porcupine.

The roadrunner (Geococcyx californianus) *is a cuckoo that seldom flies. Instead, it runs very fast on its long legs along the scrub-desert ground. A sudden chill in the air—and the roadrunner puffs way up, its feathers sticking out, looking like an avian porcupine.*

27

The raven (Corvus corax) is a glossy blue-black or purplish black bird, the largest member of the Corvidae family, which also includes crows and jays. Ravens are much larger than crows, closer to the size of hawks. To many cultures, ravens were thought of as messengers of the gods or even gods themselves. Ravens may live twenty-five years or longer in captivity.

Evermore

"Dirty. Brooding. Noisy. Road-kill pecking."
—Baltimore Sun

Dirty? No more
than a child in the park,
a worker in the mines,
a runner in the dark.

Brooding? No more
than a teen in school,
than a poet at her verse,
than a clown or a fool.

Noisy? No more
than children at play,
than a short rock concert,
than the break of day.

Road-kill pecking?
What does this mean?
An unpaid worker
keeping all roads clean.

Lost Bird: A Haiku

When the last wet place—
upland ponds, coastal marshes—
dries, good-bye, wood stork.

The wood stork (Mycteria americana) is a large wading bird that relies on touch to catch its food. Walking slowly through shallow ponds and sloughs, it holds its bill open under the water's surface. The minute a fish or frog or snake touches that bill—snap! The wood stork nests in treetop colonies. Each nesting pair needs about 440 pounds of fish during breeding season. The considerable loss of wetlands in prime wood stork territory, such as Florida, has put the bird on the endangered species list.

Wood/Peck

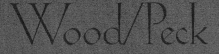

Wood	Time to
Peck	Work
Peck	Work
Peck	Work
Up the	Flick and
Bark	Fleck
Bark	Fleck
Bark	Fleck
In the	Look for
Day	Bugs
Day	Bugs
Day	Bugs
Not the	As I
Dark	Peck
Dark	Peck
Dark	Peck.

The pileated woodpecker (Dryocopus pileatus) is the largest North American woodpecker, about the size of a crow. The pileated woodpecker excavates deep holes in trees, stumps, and downed timber, searching for its insect food. Carpenter ants are a favorite, though it will also eat wood-boring beetles.